This book belongs to

_____

www.JoAnnMDickinsonAuthor.com

Library of Congress Control Number: 2022900878

ISBN: Hardcover 978-1-7378041-3-0
Paperback 978-1-7378041-5-4

The content of this work, including, but not limited to, the accuracy of events, people, and places
depicted; permission to use previously published materials including; and any advice given or actions
advocated are solely the responsibility of the author, who assumes all liability for said work and
indemnifies the publisher against any claims stemming from publication of the work.

Two Sweet Peas Publishing

Rylee
The Young
Rocketeer

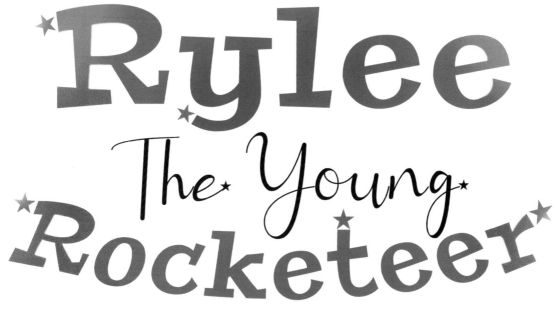

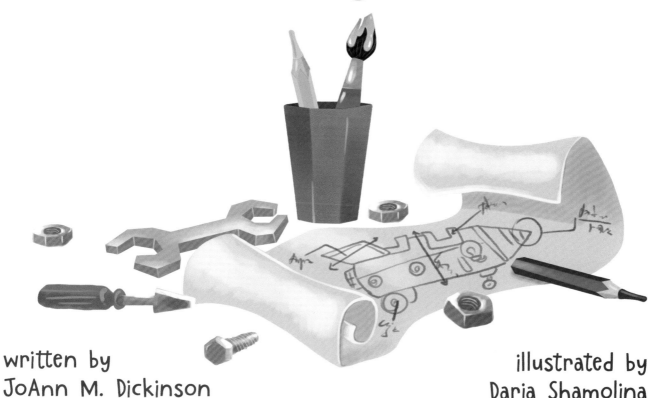

written by
JoAnn M. Dickinson

illustrated by
Daria Shamolina

I'm **Rylee**.
I build things like engines and sprockets.
To some, I'm the girl
who can build parts for **rockets**.

I want to be known as
'**The Young Rocketeer**'–
who declares, "**have no fear!**"
while I'm dressed in my gear.

So, one day, I'll become
all I'm hoping to be,
and I'd like this **decision**
to be up to me.

I would love **blasting off** through the Earth's atmosphere with the rocket I built as a skilled **rocketeer.**

I will fly in my **rocket**
throughout space and back!
My friend, **Cosmo** will ride
in the safe storage rack.

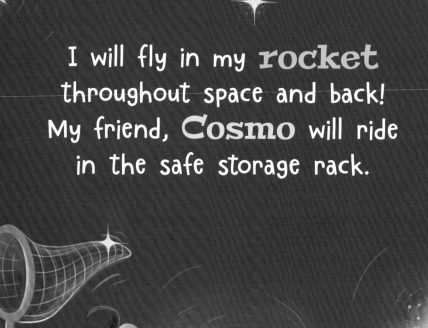

When I'm up there,
I'll gaze at the **moon** and the **stars**.
I will visit the **planets**
you can't reach with cars.

I'll blast off to the moon,
which will be so much fun—
to meet aliens and Martians.
My journey's begun!

I'll see **Mercury! Venus!**
So close to the Sun,
they're just too hot to visit—
and must weigh a ton!

Now, majestic **Earth**—
third, where it so often rains,
is fifth largest—
with mountains, deep canyons, and plains.

Planet Earth is **high-tech**
with its cars, planes, and trains.
They can be so appealing
to those with **keen** brains!

We know **Mars** is the planet
that's **fourth** from the Sun.
As my friend then explains,
"It's the red, dusty one!"

Massive **Jupiter**—fifth.
I will now blow your mind:
It has more than
the mass of all planets **combined!**

Well, the "gas giant"
Saturn's magnificent rings
and its yellowish colors
show beauty that sings.

Then, **Uranus** and **Neptune**:
"Ice Giants," they say.
They are seventh and eighth
from the Sun—far away.

It's so risky to visit them both,
as my **rocket**
could crack a head-gasket
or fracture a **socket**.

Dwarf **Pluto**:
No longer considered a planet.
From Earth, it looks small—
like a round **pomegranate**.

Our large **Solar System's**
a band of soft light
where the **stars** of the Milky Way
twinkle at night.

I observe the dark sky,
and I **dream** I'm on Mars.
As a girl in a rocket,
I'll reach for the **stars**.

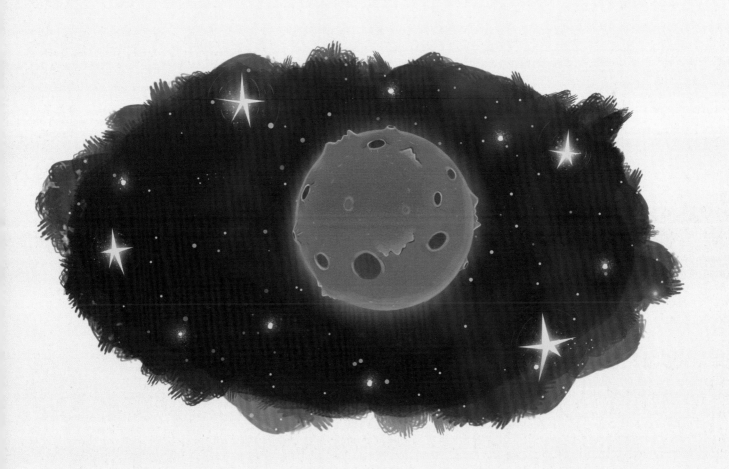

In the driver's seat,
soon I'll be **taking** my place.
I will quickly take off
to **explore** outer space!

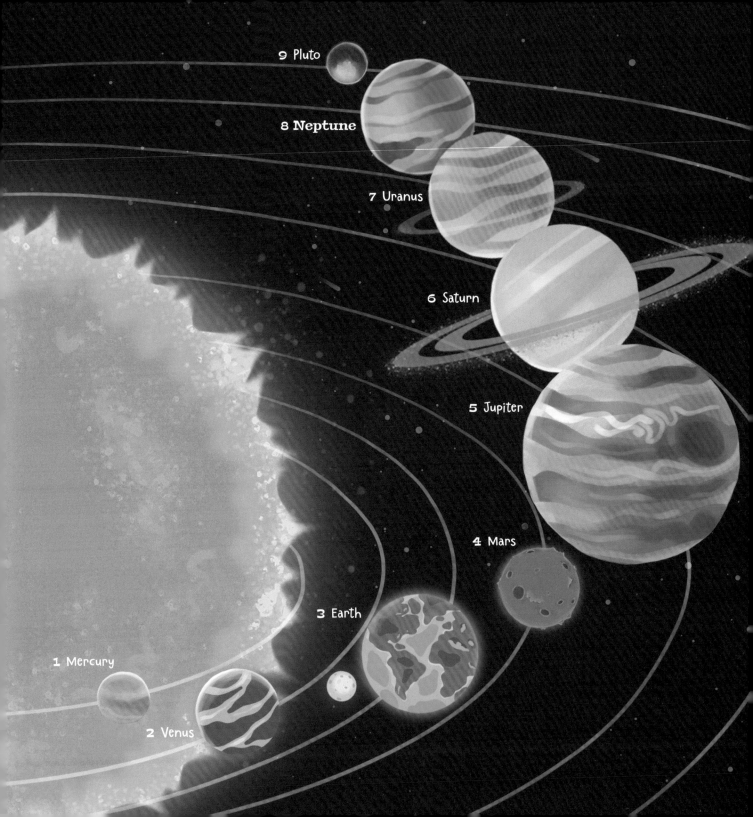

JoAnn M. Dickinson was born in Madison, Wisconsin, and moved to Southern California at a young age, where she currently resides with her husband. JoAnn is a wife, mother of one and a proud grandparent of two. She has been artistic most of her life and wrote her first book I Love To Go Camping in 2016. JoAnn started her own publishing company Two Sweet Peas Publishing in 2020 and continues to write and publish children's books. Coming soon: Lulu's New Fur Friend, John's Camping Adventures, Camping At Crab Run Beach and more new characters in the near future.

Author

Follow her website for future book release dates, appearances and other exciting information at www.JoAnnMDickinsonAuthor.com

Daria Shamolina began her illustrating adventure at the age of 14 when she was hired for her first job at a newspaper created by teenagers. She later studied at her local University and began professionally publishing. She has illustrated multiple children's books and has a special talent for creating adorable, colorful and bright characters. Daria resides in the Ukraine with her son, Daniel.

Illustrator

As an editor, **Robin Katz** loves helping authors bring their stories to life for young people! In the past two years, she has edited over one hundred fifty children's and young adult (YA) books—both rhyming and non-rhyming. With her background as a pediatric occupational therapist, social worker, and OT professor, Robin has created a unique editing approach that her clients often refer to as her 'magic touch'... hence the name Word Wiz for her editing services! When she is not editing, Robin enjoys spending quality time with her family—including her seven grandchildren.

Author

JoAnn M. Dickinson was born in Madison, Wisconsin, and moved to Southern California at a young age, where she currently resides with her husband. JoAnn is a wife, mother of one and a proud grandparent of two. She has been artistic most of her life and wrote her first book I Love To Go Camping in 2016. JoAnn started her own publishing company Two Sweet Peas Publishing in 2020 and continues to write and publish children's books. Coming soon: Lulu's New Fur Friend, John's Camping Adventures, Camping At Crab Run Beach and more new characters in the near future.

Follow her website for future book release dates, appearances and other exciting information at www.JoAnnMDickinsonAuthor.com

Illustrator

Daria Shamolina began her illustrating adventure at the age of 14 when she was hired for her first job at a newspaper created by teenagers. She later studied at her local University and began professionally publishing. She has illustrated multiple children's books and has a special talent for creating adorable, colorful and bright characters. Daria resides in the Ukraine with her son, Daniel.

As an editor, **Robin Katz** loves helping authors bring their stories to life for young people! In the past two years, she has edited over one hundred fifty children's and young adult (YA) books—both rhyming and non-rhyming. With her background as a pediatric occupational therapist, social worker, and OT professor, Robin has created a unique editing approach that her clients often refer to as her 'magic touch'... hence the name Word Wiz for her editing services! When she is not editing, Robin enjoys spending quality time with her family—including her seven grandchildren.